Sleeping Out

by Joy Cowley

What's that going o-o-o-o-o-o?

A dog.　Go to sleep.

What's that going sniffle, sniffle?

A hedgehog.   Go to sleep.

What's that going yowl, yowl?

A cat.   Go to sleep.

What's that going scratch, scratch?

A possum.   Go to sleep.

What's that going zzzz-zzzz?

It's Mom.   She's gone to sleep.